STEAMTEAM 5 CHRONICLES: MYSTERY OF THE HAUNTED CIDER MILL

GREG HELMSTETTER

PAMELA METIVIER

MONSOON PUBLISHING

Written by Greg Helmstetter & Pamela Metivier

Illustrated by Greg Helmstetter

ISBN-13: 978-0-9993187-9-9

Printed in the U.S.A.

CONTENTS

OTHER STEAMTEAM 5 BOOKS

STEAMTeam 5: The Beginning

STEAMTeam 5: Mystery at Makerspace (October 2018)

STEAMTeam 5: The Beginning - Coloring & Activity Book

Available at STEAMTeam5.com

To receive a free .PDF ebook copy of our STEAMTeam 5 Coloring & Activity book, please send an email to info@steamteam5.com and mention the title of this book.

THE FARMER'S MARKET

*A*riana loved getting up early on Saturday mornings to go with her mother to the Farmer's Market.

On this particular Saturday morning, Ariana wrote down a wish list for the perfect trip to the market: apple cider, artisan chocolate, winter squash, handmade soap, and some massive sunflowers she planned to use as inspiration for her next painting.

Apple cider was on her mother's list too. Sanders Ciders was always the first booth they visited at the market.

Sanders Ciders had been selling cider at this farmer's market for over 30 years.

"It's a tough business," Ariana's mother explained. "But everyone loves their cider."

"Good morning!" beamed Molly Sanders, the co-owner of Sanders Ciders, as Ariana and her mother got in line to buy a jug of cider.

Mark Sanders was Molly's husband and business partner. He was hurrying back and forth between the cash register and a long line of customers.

Mark was a fifth-generation cider maker. His great-great-grandfather, Winston Sanders, had started Sanders Ciders when he moved into town as a young man in the 1850s.

"Mark, Ariana's here!" Molly announced.

Mark waved to Ariana. Ariana waved and smiled back. It was so nice that the Sanders greeted each of their customers by name.

When it was Ariana's turn to order, Mark Sanders held up his index finger. "Before you order, I have a question to ask you."

"Okay," replied Ariana, curious to know what he might want.

"Come over here a second," whispered Mark, waving her over to a quiet corner of their stand.

Ariana met him, intrigued by the secrecy.

Mark looked around to make sure nobody was close enough to hear, when he spoke to Ariana.

"Molly and I are planning a town Halloween party next weekend, on Friday and Saturday nights—at our Old Cider Mill," Mark explained, trying to hide his excitement.

"Cool!" beamed Ariana. Ariana loved Halloween. It was her favorite day of the year!

"We'd like to hire you to make a banner for the party—and to design a flyer promoting the party and then post it around town," Mark continued.

"I'd love to!" Ariana exclaimed.

"Great! How does $40 sound?" said Mark.

"Fantastic!" said Ariana. "I can start right away. How about if I drop by the Old Cider Mill today to do a bit of research?"

"Perfect!" replied Mark. "We should be there all afternoon."

Ariana was so excited about her new project that she skipped away from the stand without even buying anything. Thankfully, her mother caught up with her, holding a big jug of fresh apple cider and some other treats that the Sanders had slipped into her bag.

Later that day, Ariana slid her sketch pad, her drawing pencils, and her camera into her backpack. She planned to ride her bike out to the Old Cider Mill—a big, stone building in the woods where the Sanders family had been crushing and pressing apples to make delicious apple cider for over a century.

Ariana was on a mission to come up with a creative theme for the Sanders' Halloween party.

"Witches maybe? Skeletons? Nothing with zombies. They're overused these days," she mumbled to herself as she hopped on her bike and headed over to the mill for some inspiration.

She peddled down the street and then turned off onto the lonely country road that led deep into the woods.

Autumn was in the air. The breeze had a crisp chill and the leaves were ablaze in beautiful hues of yellow, amber, and red.

Ariana loved this time of year. It was "her season," she thought to herself, mindful of her flaming red hair that seemed at home with the orange and red leaves of the forest.

The road was vaguely familiar to her. She had been out to the Old Cider Mill a few times growing up, on school field trips and on adventures with her friends. Everybody in town knew that the old mill was "haunted." Or, at least, that's what the older kids told the younger children to try and scare them during stories around the campfire.

As long as anyone could remember, it had been a local tradition for teenagers in town to drive out to the Old Cider Mill on Halloween and touch the water wheel on the side of the building at the stroke of midnight.

The rules were that you had to hold your finger on the water wheel and count to ten—and hope that the ghost of Jennylou Livingston didn't snatch you by the wrist, pull you inside, and crush your bones in the cider press!

Ariana chuckled at this silliness. Every small town needs its ghost story, she thought. Of course, she didn't actually believe any of it.

Still, she herself had never been to the mill at midnight, and she imagined it would be pretty scary to be out there in the woods, counting to ten, waiting to feel a cold, white hand clench her by the wrist!

The thought sent a chill down her spine and she got goosebumps. "Must be the cold air," she thought, trying to reassure herself.

She started to realize that these woods were actually kind of spooky. Worse, the Old Cider Mill was nowhere to be seen.

THE OLD CIDER MILL

"Where is it?" wondered Ariana. She had been riding longer than she had expected, and still all she saw was more woods. The woods grew darker the deeper she rode into them.

At last, she rounded a bend in the road and spotted the Old Cider Mill in the distance. She exhaled loudly, feeling a little relieved.

The building was a very old, grayish-brown stone building with the name "Sanders Ciders" painted on the front of it in white letters.

The paint had partly worn off over the years, but that didn't really matter. Everyone knew it was the original home of the best cider in the state.

On one side of the building, there was an old wooden water mill. It looked like a giant gear. The wheel was not turning.

Ariana hopped off her bike near the entrance of the main building. She leaned it against a green picnic table nearby.

She looked around, noticing that she was alone. All she could hear was the clinking of a few wind chimes and the cool autumn breeze making the tops of the golden aspen trees dance and glitter in the sunlight.

She paused briefly to breathe in the fresh fall air, then she opened the front door. A bell rang loudly to announce her.

"Hi, Ariana!" Molly cheered from the other side of the entry-way. "Sorry about the loud bell!" she added, trying not to laugh.

"Mark had to run out for a bit but come on in!"

Molly was wearing an apron. She wiped her hands on it before reaching out to greet Ariana with a firm handshake.

"We're so excited to work with you! You did such a good job on the signage for Lillian's dance studio!" Molly beamed.

"Thanks!" replied Ariana, smiling ear to ear. She loved working with local businesses.

Ariana scanned the room. It was decorated with old antiques and the center of the room was filled with shelves containing every type of apple product you can imagine: applesauce, apple butter, apple jam... even apple soap! And, of course, lots of apple cider.

The room smelled sweet and a little musty. It reminded her of her great-grandmother's house during the holidays. A fire was burning in the big stone fireplace. The memories brought a smile to her face.

"I just love this building," Ariana said. "It has so much texture. It's like walking back in time."

"This building is over 150 years old," Molly explained.

"It definitely feels old," Ariana replied. "Like it's got stories to tell. It's kinda creepy—in a cool way!"

Molly laughed. "You're not the only one who's noticed that! Yes, it certainly has a certain feeling when you enter it."

"In fact," Molly added. "There are legends about this old mill being haunted."

Ariana's eyes lit up. "Oh, I've heard all about that!" she said. "Every kid who grows up in Portsbury has heard about it."

"Yes, I'll bet they have!" Molly said with a smile. "The kids like to come at Halloween and dare each other to touch the water wheel.

"We don't mind, it's all good fun," Molly continued. "But just between you and me, it sure would be fun to jump out and scare them one of those nights!"

Ariana giggled in delight as she imagined big, tough teenagers screaming like little babies and running away. "I would pay money to see that!" she said.

Ariana wanted to ask Molly something, but she paused. She was not quite sure if it was appropriate.

"What is it?" asked Molly.

"Well..." said Ariana, "I was just wondering..."

Ariana was hesitant to continue, but she did anyway. "Have you ever seen anything strange happen here? You know, the..."

"Ghost?" asked Molly.

Ariana nodded.

Molly suddenly looked a little more serious. Ariana bit her lip, hoping she hadn't offended her.

"Well every old building has its creaks and groans when the wind blows hard," Molly said. "Mark believes it's haunted—he grew up here, you know."

Ariana nodded. She knew Mark's family went way back.

"He always talked about seeing something move out of the corner of the eye, and such," Molly explained. "What a fun place for a child—they have such active imaginations."

Ariana nodded.

"As for me," Molly continued, "I've heard some strange noises at night, but I've never actually seen anything too strange. I will say, the building does have this kind of... energy to it. Hard to explain."

Ariana nodded again.

"But what I can tell you," Molly continued, "is that there is a *reason* this Old Cider Mill has a reputation for being haunted."

Ariana's eyes grew wide and she held her breath in anticipation.

"Would you like to hear about it?"

Ariana nodded eagerly.

"Well, then, why don't we sit down by the fireplace and we'll enjoy a couple mugs of hot, spiced cider."

Ariana nodded excitedly again and smiled as Molly poured two steaming mugs of cider from an insulated carafe.

The two sunk down into comfortable chairs by the crackling fire that burned in the old stone fireplace.

Molly paused for a moment and looked into the fire as though thinking about where to begin. Finally, she looked at Ariana and spoke.

"Something happened here a long time ago. Something terrible."

THE LEGEND OF JENNYLOU LIVINGSTON

*M*olly Sanders took a long sip of steaming spiced cider as the fire in the fireplace popped and crackled. Ariana had never been more excited to hear any story in her life.

"As the legend goes," Molly Sanders began, "this land already had acres and acres of apple trees when Winston Sanders arrived here in the 1850s. He drove his wagon all the way here from Springfield, Ohio.

"He showed up with his wagon, his tools, a brand-new cast iron cider mill, and his new wife," Molly explained.

"And big dreams!" Molly blurted. "Did you know, the two of them built the building you're sitting in with their own two hands?!"

Ariana's eyes lit up. "Was Winston's wife Jennylou Livingston? The ghost?"

"Good heavens, no!" replied Molly with a grimace. "Jennylou Livingston lived in the woods nearby, all by herself."

"She had long white hair and was mean – *really* mean— mean as a badger stuck under a fence!" Molly continued.

"She was nothing but trouble from the first day Winston Sanders and his bride arrived," Molly added, shaking her head.

"What kind of trouble?" asked Ariana.

"Well, for starters," Molly continued, "Jennylou would appear out of the woods and just scream and scream, 'Get off my land! Get off my land!' She had no legal claim to the land, but she couldn't be reasoned with.

"And then, after Winston and Becky – that was his wife's name. After they built the built the first mill house, strange things started to happen."

"What kind of things?" asked Ariana.

"Strange things. Terrible screams coming from the woods in the middle of the night. Then livestock would just disappear. Or turn up dead. They could never prove Jennylou had anything to do with it—might have been a wild animal, the local sheriff said."

Molly paused to take a sip of cider. Ariana was impatient to hear what happened next.

"After their first harvest," Molly continued, "the Sanders started selling their cider in town. It was a big hit! Becky had a baby, and things were going really well. That is, until..."

Ariana's eyes opened wide...

"The Sanders woke up one night to the smell of smoke. The mill house was engulfed in flames! They desperately tried to put out the fire, but it was too late. They got away safe with their baby, but the entire building burned to the ground."

"Oh my!" exclaimed Ariana. "What did they do?"

"They did what all hearty folk do when they get knocked down," said Molly, with a faraway look in her eyes. Then she looked right at Ariana.

"They did whatever they needed to do to get back up on their feet. They had grit. They were survivors. So, they rebuilt. They had lost everything. Everything, that is, except the big, heavy cast iron parts of the cider press. They dug 'em up right out of the ashes. Winston built his cider press back into perfect working order, fashioned all the wood parts himself, from memory."

Ariana looked on in amazement.

Molly continued. "And then he built a new building, bigger this time. And out of stone, so it couldn't burn as easily. That's the building you're sitting in right now."

"Wow," murmured Ariana, looking around at the building as though really seeing it for the first time. "That's so inspiring!"

"But that's not the end of the story," said Molly.

"Winston and Becky vowed never to let anything like that happen again."

Ariana nodded quietly in agreement.

"So, Winston rode his horse deep into the woods and found Jennylou, and told her, 'If you so much as touch one finger to my building, it'll be the end of your tortured days,'" Molly hissed.

"Wow," said Ariana. "What did Jennylou say?"

"According to the legend," Molly continued, "Jennylou just screamed like she always did. Screamed over and over, 'Get out! Get out!' And Winston rode away on his horse.

"Now, according to him, that was the end of it. He told people she must've left town, because nobody ever saw her again," said Molly, before taking a sip of her cider.

"According to him?" Ariana asked, curious.

"That's right," said Molly. "But most folks think there's more to it.

You see, after the fire, Winston had taken to sleeping outside every night in a chair, with a shotgun, to protect his new cider mill."

Ariana started twitching in her seat. This is the part she had been waiting for.

Molly continued. "One night, Winston had to leave town on urgent business. Now, Becky, she was just as tough as him, grew up on the prairie, and she took his place that night outside guarding the mill—shotgun on one side, her baby on the other, swaddled in the cradle.

"Who knows what's true and what's not even last week, let alone a hundred and fifty years ago, but as the legend goes..."

Molly paused to take one last gulp of the cider from her mug while Ariana tried not to burst from anticipation.

"Legend goes, Becky woke up suddenly that night when a cold hand grabbed her by the wrist.

"She opened her eyes and found herself staring face-to-face, straight into Jennylou's eyes, black like coal. And, for the first time ever, Jennylou didn't scream. She just whispered right into Becky's face, *I told you to get out. But you didn't listen. And now I'm going to crush your bones.*'"

"And before Becky had a chance to collect her wits or grab the shotgun, Jennylou yanked Becky up out of her chair by the wrist and dragged her straight to the cellar door."

Ariana gasped. "That's awful! What happened next?"

"Well, like I said, Becky was hearty stock and could take care of herself. Just as Jennylou dragged her to the top of the cellar stairs, Becky grabbed hold of the doorway and wriggled and kicked herself free.

"In the struggle, Jennylou lost her footing and went tumbling headfirst down the stairs.

She hit the ground and broke her neck. And that was the end of Jennylou Livingston."

"That's the scariest thing I've ever heard!" said Ariana.

Molly nodded. "That little baby in the cradle was Cyrus Sanders—Mark's great grandfather. His mama, Becky, told him that story when he was grown up. Nobody knows if it's true."

"Do you think it's true?" asked Ariana.

"Hard to say. To the rest of the world, Jennylou just up and disappeared. That wasn't so strange—there was never any investigation. Nobody ever found a body. But..."

Ariana leaned forward as Molly paused to choose her words carefully.

"Some folks say Becky had a particularly lovely garden the following spring," said Molly with a little mischievous smile.

Ariana gasped.

"Or maybe," Molly went on, "maybe Jennylou never even came by that night. Or maybe Becky chased her off with her shotgun and she ran off into the woods, never to be seen again. Or, I should say, not for a hundred years, when folks started telling the kids ghost stories about how they'd caught a glimpse of old Jennylou with her long, white hair, wandering deep in the woods, wrapped head-to-toe in torn up scraps of cheesecloth.

"Nobody knows. But regardless of what actually happened to Jennylou, it's a good story. I don't know if her ghost explains the strange things people have seen, or the creaks and groans of this old building on stormy nights, but it sure gives the local kids something scary to talk about!"

"It sure does!" said Ariana, a bit unnerved herself.

The two sat in silence for a moment.

"Now," said Molly, "about that Halloween banner and the flyers. Mark said you wanted to do some research."

"Yes!" said Ariana. She had been so engrossed in Molly's story that she had almost forgotten why she was there.

"I was hoping to look around and get some ideas for a theme for the design."

"Would you like to take a tour?" Molly asked.

"Absolutely!" said Ariana.

"Splendid," said Molly. "And at the end of the tour, there's something very special I'd like to show you. Something that might give you lots of ideas for your design!"

4

THE SANDERS FARM

"Right this way," Molly said as she led Ariana out the front door.

She led Ariana out back to a modern building. Molly slid open a large metal garage door and flipped a switch, turning on a bank of bright fluorescent lights.

In the center of the building was a large, stainless steel machine. Ariana had never seen a machine like it before. It was not what she imagined an apple mill would look like. It had tubes running out of it and even had a small set of stairs attached to it.

On top of the machine was a gigantic funnel. Beside the machine sat an enormous bin filled with an entire truckload of apples.

"This is our new pneumatic fruit press!" Molly beamed as she pulled a handkerchief from a pocket on her apron and wiped a tiny smudge off the side of the gleaming, steel machine.

"This is amazing! How does it work?" asked Ariana, as she removed her camera's lens cover and began snapping photos of the machine.

"It all starts with the apples," Molly said, pointing to the large bin. "We've always handpicked our apples—and only once they're ripe." She had a note of pride in her voice.

"First we pick and wash the fruit. Then we dump the apples down this chute," Molly explained. She demonstrated how the mill worked by pretending to drop an apple down the funnel part on top of the mill.

"This mill grinds the apples into a pulp. The pulp is called *mash*. The mash moves down this conveyor into the press, which uses a giant air bag – it's like a balloon – to squeeze out the juice," she continued.

"So, this machine presses all of the juice out of the mash?" Ariana asked.

"You've got it!" Molly exclaimed.

"Using an air bag? That's fascinating," said Ariana. "I never would've imagined."

Then Ariana thought to herself, that's exactly the kind of invention her friend, Evelyn, would think up to squeeze juice out of pulp. Evelyn was known for inventing machines to solve problems. She was an amazing engineer, and Ariana couldn't wait to tell her about this apple cider machine.

"It's a very efficient process, and it will save us a ton of time," said Molly. "But the machine was very expensive," she sighed.

"I love it!" Ariana cooed as she bent down on one knee to capture a photo from a unique angle.

Ariana stood up and took in a long, deep breath. "It smells so good in here," she said.

"It sure does," Molly replied. "But you should smell it when it's actually running... you'll start dreaming of applesauce!"

Molly led Ariana out of the building and showed her around the rest of the property. She pointed out the orchards full of trees just bursting with apples, a pumpkin patch with a scarecrow, the old mill pond that routed water through a sluice to the old water mill, and several other new pieces of equipment the Sanders had recently purchased to modernize their business.

"These are amazing machines!" Ariana said as they walked back toward the old stone building with the store inside.

"They sure are," Molly replied.

"They'll pay for themselves over time, but we need to sell a lot of cider this season to make sure we can make the payments on them."

"I see," Ariana replied.

"It's a big risk. If we don't make our payments, we could lose the property," Molly said anxiously.

"But it's been in your family for years!" Ariana cried.

"Yes, for five generations," Molly agreed. "But we have a plan. And that's why you're here!"

Ariana tilted her head to listen intently.

Molly began to explain her plan. "We want to throw the Halloween party of all Halloween parties! We plan to do it every year. So, this will be the 'First Annual Sanders Cider Halloween Party,' and we want to make a really big splash!"

Ariana smiled. She was excited to play a role in the mission.

"And, at this party," Molly continued, "we plan to announce a new line of apple fizzy drinks!"

"Ooooh, that sounds amazing!" Ariana cheered, as they walked up to the old stone mill house.

"And now, before I let you loose to run around and take your pictures and get your inspiration... as I promised, I'd like to show you something really special," said Molly.

"What is it!?" asked Ariana.

"It's the heart and soul of our whole family business: The original cast iron cider mill that Winston Sanders drove in his wagon all the way from Ohio."

"It's the one he watched burn to the ground, and then rebuilt it, and ran it for the rest of his long life.

He made thousands and thousands of gallons of cider and made the Sanders name and farm famous in these parts."

"Wow! You still have it?" asked Ariana.

"Yes," said Molly, "we sure do. It hasn't run in decades. Mark's grandfather, Cyrus Sanders, upgraded to a diesel press in the 1920s during prohibition. The water wheel is real, but it's just for decoration these days. I don't think it's worked since the 70s, but, you know, it's a local landmark and an icon of our whole business. Can't have an Old Cider Mill without a water wheel, right?" she said, cheerfully.

"No, I guess you can't," Ariana agreed. "Is the wheel still connected to the old cider press?"

"Yes, it is," said Molly. "Here, follow me. The press is down in the cellar. One of these days we'll clean it up and get it running again."

"That way, we can demonstrate how it works to the kids who come on school field trips. Never enough hours in the day, though."

"Here's the cellar door," Molly said, as she leaned down and opened the old, creaky, wooden doors.

Ariana craned her neck to peek inside. The steps disappeared into darkness. Beyond that, she couldn't see a thing. The cellar was pitch black.

Just then, Molly's cell phone rang. She answered it. "Hi, hon. Yep. Uh-huh. Ok, sure thing. Okay, see you soon. Bye-bye."

Molly turned to Ariana. "I'm sorry dear, but Mark needs me to bring him our truck. Looks like he's bought another piece of machinery."

"Oh, no problem," said Ariana.

"Please feel free to look around," said Molly as she started walking toward the parking lot. "Anywhere you like... watch your step down in the cellar, it's a bit messy. Take all the pictures you want. I'm sure you'll come up with something great for the party!"

"I'll sure do my best!" said Ariana.

Molly opened the door to her pickup truck and called over to Ariana. "I should be back in about 45 minutes!"

Ariana smiled and nodded, then waved goodbye as Molly

started the engine and drove off into the distance. Seconds later, Ariana could no longer see or hear the truck, and all was quiet. She stood there, next to Old Cider Mill, all alone.

5

ALL ALONE

"Where to start...?" Ariana wondered to herself. She returned to the cellar door and paused for several seconds. She took a deep breath then pulled the door open cautiously and peered into the darkness. It was still pitch black. She couldn't see a thing.

Ariana used her hand to shield her eyes from the afternoon sun, and squinted, trying to see anything at all. All she could see was darkness.

"I'm sure there's a light switch inside," she thought. "Or my eyes will adjust once I'm down there."

Suddenly, a realization dawned on Ariana. Steps led down into the cellar. Was that really how Jennylou Livingston met her end? "Creepy!" Ariana said out loud at the thought.

She looked again into the blackness and realized something. That she was afraid.

"Silly girl, what are you afraid of?" Ariana said out loud to herself, laughing a little. "Spooked by a ghost story? Afraid that a vengeful Jennylou is going to snatch me by the wrist and crush my bones? Ha!"

Feeling momentarily brave, Ariana was about to step down into the blackness of the cellar, when the wind suddenly picked up, rustling the aspen leaves. The wind chimes nearby clinked louder than before. Just then, she heard a low, deep groaning sound coming from the cellar. Or was it a creak? She wasn't sure.

"The water wheel!" said Ariana. She realized the wheel might move a little whenever a strong wind blows and send creaking sounds running through the whole building. Yes, that must be it! "Nothing to be afraid of, right?" she told herself.

The wind blew again, harder this time. Again, she heard the deep, groaning sound, like the whole building was moaning in agony.

"Yeahhh... no," said Ariana. "So many other things to look at around here. Beautiful stuff!

"I need to get pictures of the outside of the building from a distance while the light is good, right?" she convinced herself.

She decided that investigating the cellar could wait until Molly returned. Ariana could easily kill 45 minutes walking around, taking pictures and doing a couple of sketches.

Ariana made her way back into the store, where Molly had told her the Jennylou story by the fireplace. The fire had gone out.

Not a lot of people visited the store. Most people bought their Sanders Cider and apple pies at the farmer's market or at the grocery store.

Still, the Sanders kept a small inventory in the store just in case they got some foot traffic from locals, or the occasional tour group.

Ariana took several photos inside the store. She looked at the LCD display on her camera. She frowned a bit.

"Looks like a brochure," she thought. "Applesauce just isn't very scary. Maybe I can get some spooky Halloweenish pictures outside in the apple orchard."

She set out to explore the apple trees behind the Old Mill.

Ariana walked between the rows of trees, shuffling through small piles of brown, orange and red leaves that had fallen along her path. She loved the damp, earthy smell of leaves but resisted the urge to roll around in them. After all, she was on a mission.

As she made a new path through the leaves, she looked up to admire the stark, creepy-looking branches that were blocking out the sun above. They crackled under the pressure of the wind.

Click, click, click – went the sound of her camera shutter. She must have taken a dozen photos of one branch alone.

"Now this is more like it. So creepy. I love it," she cooed as she made her way back to the main building.

"Let's see... what next?..."

All of a sudden, she spotted the water wheel on the front of the building.

"Yes! The water wheel! Of course!" she rejoiced. "I almost forgot!"

She rushed toward the water wheel with her pencil and sketch book in hand. The water wheel was on the label on all Sanders Cider jugs.

Ariana started looking for angles, or distortions, she could make that would transform the water wheel symbol from something friendly and wholesome into something a little more sinister and spooky-looking.

After drawing for a while, she was quite happy with her work. She slipped her sketchpad into her backpack.

Ariana looked at her phone to see what time it was. Molly was past due.

"It's getting late," Ariana thought. "Maybe she'll pull up at any moment... or maybe she got delayed. Either way, I need to be getting home soon."

Ariana really wanted to see the old press down in the cellar. Like Molly said, it was the "heart and soul" of the company.

"Who knows," Ariana said, talking out loud to herself, "it might even become the centerpiece of my design."

She walked back over to the open cellar door. The sun was lower in the sky now and with less glare, she could see a little better into the blackness. She could make out the shape of the stairs heading down, at least.

"Welp, here goes... it's cellar time!" Ariana announced as she headed down the steps.

6

INTO THE CELLAR

*A*riana reached out and felt a handrail on the cellar staircase. She used it to carefully guide herself down the stairs. As she descended a few concrete steps, she found herself standing in a pitch black, cold, damp space. The room smelled musty.

Still holding onto the handrail, she reached her other hand out to feel for a light switch.

"Aaaaaa!" she screamed as she realized she had just reached into a thick crackling spiderweb.

"Enough of this!" thought Ariana. "I need some light. She wished she had one of her STEAMTeam 5 friends with her.

"What would Evelyn do if she were here and didn't have a

flashlight?" Ariana asked herself. Evelyn could solve almost any problem using nothing but her multi-tool and a stick of chewing gum.

"I don't even chew gum," thought Ariana. "Besides, what I really need is a light."

"If only... WAIT!... Of course!" Ariana remembered that she had her phone with her. She quickly pulled it out of her pocket and fumbled to turn it on in flashlight mode.

At last, Ariana could see her immediate surroundings in the cellar.

The room was lined with shelves containing a bunch of old wooden casks, a few large pumpkins, an assortment of old, rusty tools, and other odds and ends.

On the floor were many stacks of crates full of apples.

She shined her phone's light up toward the ceiling. There were thick, wooden beams caked in dusty cobwebs. "Ew," she thought. And there it was, hanging between two of the beams: a single light bulb.

"Ah-ha!" cried Ariana. She ran her phone's flashlight along the wire leading from the light fixture in the ceiling, along one of the beams, down the wall, to a light switch near the door, hidden in the shadows.

"There you are," she said as she flipped the switch.

The light bulb turned on, but it was not very bright. Still, Ariana could now see more of the cellar than before. She saw a filing cabinet, an old writer's desk, and in the back corner of the cellar, there it was: Winston Sanders' original cast iron cider press.

Ariana turned on her camera's flash and snapped some photos. She then moved in for a closer look.

The antique apple press was a work of art, with stylish decorations adorning its cast iron parts. Like a smaller version of the stainless-steel machine Ariana had seen earlier that day, the antique press had a large, funnel-shaped hopper at the top for pouring apples into the blades that would grind them into apple mash.

The mash would then be scooped onto sheets of cheesecloth, which were folded and placed under a solid block of oak that the machine would press down under tremendous pressure, squeezing out all the juice into buckets. Both the grinding blades and the press were powered by a big iron wheel that was connected to a system of well-worn belts and pulleys that ran up toward the ceiling.

Ariana used the light from her phone to look up at where they led.

"Whoa!" Ariana blurted. The belts were connected to a thick, iron axle that was connected to the water wheel on the outside of the old stone building.

She marveled at how it all must have looked when it functioned a hundred years ago!

Ariana drew a quick sketch of the old press and took a few more photos. As she moved in to get a closer look, she noticed something she hadn't seen before: a lever with a sign that read "pull me" hanging on it.

"Okay, I will!" she announced, as she reached over and pulled the lever without hesitation.

Just then, she felt an intense chill come over her, and the hairs stood up on her arms. She was suddenly freezing!

The building began to groan, louder than ever this time and the belts and pulleys slowly started turning. The iron wheel on the press started to turn, and it started to make a loud mechanical noise—kachung, kachung, kachung.

Ariana shrieked and jumped backwards, terrified that she had somehow accidentally started this ancient machine. But what happened next would defy everything she ever believed about the world!

Ariana strained to hear a sound, something faint, almost inaudible over the loud kachung kachung of the machine. It sounded like a whisper... 'get... out.'

"What was that?" thought Ariana. Was she hearing things? Was her mind playing tricks on her? There it was again! Louder this time... 'Get... Out.'

Ariana panicked... should she try to stop the machine? Should she run for her life?

Who was making that whispering sound? It was getting louder!

And as her mind raced, trying to decide what to do, an unearthly bluish glow started to emerge from the shadows. The voice became louder, and the glow took the form of a cloud of fog, and then, she couldn't believe her eyes!

Staring into the glowing fog, Ariana became almost hypnotized by a rhythmic, fluid motion. Was it... billowing white cloth? And are those two arms? And a face! With two hollow eyes and surrounded by long, tangled white hair.

Ariana screamed and backed away, clumsily feeling for the stairs behind her. She had to get out!

Suddenly, the face became fierce-looking and filled with rage and screamed a shrill "GET OUT! GET OUT!" and seemed to start lunging toward Ariana.

Something deep inside Ariana kicked in and she knew she must get away.

But in a stroke of extraordinary bravery, she raised her camera and snapped a photo of the ghostly apparition. A bright flash from the camera filled the room with light for a split second as Ariana shuffled backwards, scrambled up the stairs, and ran away from the building as fast as she could.

Within seconds, she was on her bike and pedaling at top speed up the road, headed back toward town, without ever stopping once to look behind her.

Ariana pedaled and pedaled and pedaled. At last, when she finally put some serious distance between herself and the Old Cider Mill, she skidded to a stop and nervously looked back at the road behind her. Her heart was racing, and she panted to catch her breath.

But the forest around here was completely calm. No screaming ghosts chasing her. The low sunlight still shone through the autumn leaves, and she saw a few of them fall delicately to the ground, as a pair of yellow butterflies flitted about.

"What *WAS* that?" Ariana said out loud.

She resumed pedaling home. It was not until she reached her own street that she realized she had left her sketchbook in the cellar. But sketches were no longer the most important thing on her mind. After all, she had almost just had her bones crushed by an angry phantom.

The moment Ariana reached her driveway, she pulled out her phone and typed a message to her fellow STEAMTeam 5 members:

CODE RED: I JUST SAW A GHOST!

7

STEAMTEAM 5: TO THE RESCUE!

One by one, the members of STEAMTeam 5 arrived at Ariana's house. They retreated to her bedroom, eager to learn why Ariana had called an emergency meeting about seeing a ghost.

They all began talking at once.

"What do you mean, a ghost?!" exclaimed Sandia, STEAMTeam 5's scientist.

Ariana retold the entire story about Jennylou Livingston to the others. She also explained how she came to be down in the cellar.

"This seems statistically unlikely," said Mattie, the group's mathematician. "What are the chances you'd see a ghost on your first visit to the cellar?"

"There's no such thing as ghosts," Evelyn said flatly.

"I love the idea of a ghost," said Treeka, the technologist and computer hacker extraordinaire. "This is the coolest thing that's happened all day!"

"Walk us through exactly what you saw," Sandia said to Ariana, taking out her notepad and clicking the top of her ballpoint pen.

"Okay," Ariana began. She was much more relaxed now, as she sipped a warm cup of chamomile tea.

"So, there was a lever on the old apple press down in the cellar with a sign that said 'pull me' on it," Ariana began.

"Seriously?" Evelyn asked. "It said 'pull me'?"

"Yes," Ariana confirmed. "So, I—"

"Pulled it, of course," Mattie answered.

"Yes," Ariana replied.

They all nodded. Every one of them would have done the same thing.

"And when I pulled it, this freaky, super scary ghost appeared and started screaming at me to go away!" Ariana continued.

"Dang..." Treeka replied. "That's O.P."

"What's O.P.?" asked Ariana.

"Over-powered," said Treeka.

"Ah. Yes. It was, as you say... O.P.," Ariana offered.

"So, this 'ghost,'" Sandia said, using air quotes. "What did it look like?"

"It was wearing a long white dress and had this long, crazy, wiry white hair flying everywhere," Ariana described as she waved her hands around her head.

"Modern science has made folklore about ghosts pretty outdated," said Sandia. "But... the possibility of inter-dimensional travel hasn't been disproven," she added. "Maybe you opened an Einstein-Rosen Bridge to another dimension!"

"A what?" Evelyn asked.

"A wormhole!" Sandia answered, cheerfully.

"So..." Ariana hesitated, "you're saying I opened a wormhole... with a cider press?"

Sandia's perky smile faded. "Well when you put it that way, probably not."

"Since the universe is statistically likely to be a simulation," Mattie chimed in, "perhaps Ariana witnessed a glitch in the matrix!"

"Some historians think the Salem Witch hysteria was caused by eating ergot fungus, which can cause hallucinations," Evelyn said.

"I don't even like mushrooms," Ariana replied.

They all looked at Treeka, and the room fell silent. She hadn't yet offered a hypothesis. Finally, she spoke.

"Maybe it was a ghost."

The room went silent again.

"I wish we had some evidence—no offense," Sandia sighed.

"Oh, wait!" Ariana blurted. "I can't believe I forgot in my panic to get home. I took a picture!"

"Now we're talkin'!" said Sandia, shaking her fists with excitement.

Ariana turned on her camera and turned it around for all to see. An image displayed on the screen. They all leaned forward to get a close look.

Unfortunately, the entire image was nothing but a big white blur.

"Oh, no!" cried Ariana. It's over exposed.

They all groaned, dropping their shoulders in disappointment.

"So close!" Evelyn sighed. She had just convinced herself to consider the evidence despite not believing in ghosts.

"Wait!" Ariana shrieked. "Photos often contain more information in them than the human eye can see!"

Ariana ejected the memory card from her camera and slid it into a slot on her computer nearby.

"I just need to adjust the levels in the image's histogram," she continued, as she opened the photo and began to edit it.

The girls all stared at the image on Ariana's computer screen while she adjusted the controls.

And suddenly, right before their eyes, a vague impression of a fierce-looking woman's face began to take form.

"That's who I saw!" Ariana exclaimed.

The girls all saw it too, plain as day, right there on Ariana's computer screen. Their jaws dropped.

A chill filled the room. Mattie crossed her hands over her body to warm her arms. Sandia cleared her throat nervously. Evelyn's eyes darted around the room, scanning it for signs of unwanted guests. "Consider my gaskets blown," she said.

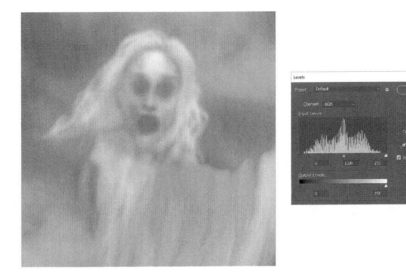

Treeka spoke softly. "Yeah, that looks like a ghost to me."

They all nodded a silent response.

8

THE SCIENTIFIC METHOD

*T*en minutes later, all five of the girls were nervously drinking cups of warm chamomile tea. They were clearly in uncharted territory for STEAMTeam 5.

"Is anybody else sort of totally freaking out?" Mattie asked the group.

"Yes. I love it," said Treeka. The others nodded, too.

Sandia paced back and forth in Ariana's room, deep in thought.

They were all familiar with Sandia's process for answering questions and solving problems. She used the *scientific method*, which involves following a series of steps:

1. Make an observation (identify the problem you want to solve or the question you want to answer).
2. Form a hypothesis (make an educated guess).
3. Test the hypothesis (conduct an experiment).
4. Draw a conclusion (analyze the data).
5. Repeat steps 1-4 as needed.

At last, Sandia stopped pacing, and spoke. "We want to know what Ariana saw near the old apple press. And we've seen a photo of what looks like a ghost."

"Now, in order to test our hypothesis that Ariana saw a ghost," Sandia continued, "I propose we all go to the Old Cider Mill to make observations."

"Clues!" Evelyn cheered.

"Yes!" Sandia answered. "

"Good idea, I'm in," said Treeka.

"Yup," Mattie agreed.

"You know I'm in," added Evelyn.

Ariana grimaced. "I... can't."

"*What?!*" the others roared in unison.

"It'll be okay, I promise," Sandia said. "That mean ghost can't grab us all by the wrist if we stick together like a team!"

"Oh, no, it's not that," said Ariana. "I'd love to go back with our whole squad and figure out what I saw.

"But I promised the Sanders I'd email them a design for their Halloween party banner tonight so they can review it," Ariana explained. "And they want me to distribute the flyers around town tomorrow, so I'll be busy all day."

"What if we help you pass out the flyers in the morning, and then we can go out to the Old Cider Mill afterwards?" Mattie suggested.

"Really? That would be great!" said Ariana.

"Yes!" Sandia cheered.

They all agreed to meet the following morning. When the others had left, Ariana returned to her room and began designing the banner for the Sanders' Halloween party.

With all the excitement, she hadn't even thought about the project. What should she feature in the design... witches? Scarecrows? Bats?

"Of course!" said Ariana. The answer had *literally* been staring her in the face. She sat down at her computer and started clicking away, creating her marketing masterpiece.

THE NEXT MORNING, THE GIRLS MET AT ARIANA'S HOUSE AT

9:00am on the nose. They rang the doorbell. Ariana opened the door.

"I can't wait to see the flyers!" said Mattie.

"Show us!" Sandia pleaded.

Ariana led them to the kitchen table, where the flyers for the Halloween party were stacked into five piles. The girls each picked one up to take a look.

The flyer looked like a small version of a movie poster, but it promoted the upcoming First Annual Sanders Cider Halloween Party. The artwork on the flyer featured a spooky version of the mill house, with a scary-looking ghost flying out of it. The ghost bore a striking resemblance to...

"Jennylou Livingston!" cried Mattie.

Ariana just smiled.

"Wow! Well done," said Treeka.

"This is cool!" Evelyn agreed.

"I'd definitely go to something like this party. It looks fun," Sandia added.

"The perfect amount of scary," Mattie chimed in.

"Great! I'm glad you all like it!," said Ariana. "The Sanders approved the design last night, and I printed them this morning."

"Did you mention the ghost?" asked Treeka.

"No," said Ariana. I figured we should stick to the plan and gather more observations first."

Ariana picked up a stack of flyers. "Everyone grab a pile, and let's head down to Main Street to start passing them around!"

"Let's do this!" Sandia cheered, picking up a stack.

ARIANA AND HER FRIENDS WALKED AROUND THE SMALL, TREE-lined town, taping flyers in store windows and handing them out to everyone they encountered.

Sandia paused near a group of college students drinking coffee outside the cafe.

"You won't want to miss this!" she said, as she handed a flyer to one of them.

"Oh, I love Sanders Cider," the young woman remarked as she examined it. "Looks fun!"

Sandia nodded in agreement, then turned to notice that her friends were waiting for her at a crosswalk. She jogged over to join them.

They were having a conversation about the ghost mystery and their mission to solve it.

"I think we should just come out and ask Mr. and Mrs. Sanders about the ghost," Evelyn suggested.

"You mean, just say, 'Hey, did you know that there's a mean ghost in your basement?" Mattie asked.

"Basically," Evelyn replied.

"Well, Molly did say that some people have seen some things," said Ariana.

"It's odd that she'd mention that and then, like twenty minutes later, you saw a ghost," said Treeka.

"Yeah, it is weird," Ariana agreed. "Especially after Molly said she's never seen anything too strange herself.

"She also mentioned that they're worried about paying for all of their new equipment," Ariana murmured.

"Hmm," Treeka thought, raising one eyebrow, as she did whenever something perplexed her. "You don't think..."

"That someone faked it?" Evelyn interjected.

"There's a famous type of crime," Treeka explained, "where someone fakes a ghost to scare off customers so they can buy property cheap from the financially distressed owners, to develop the land into luxury condominiums."

The others just stared at her.

"It's always the greedy real estate developers," Treeka added.

Evelyn squinted skeptically at Treeka.

"That's not a famous type of crime," said Evelyn. "It's the plot of literally every episode of Scooby Doo."

Treeka paused to consider that thought. "Yeah, that might be where I heard of it."

"Personally, I think we need more data before we talk to anyone about this," Sandia insisted. "But if they're up to any shenanigans, I'm worried they'll become suspicious when we start poking around, looking for clues."

"I've got it!" Mattie shouted.

"Instead of inspecting the Sanders' cellar this afternoon, instead, I'm thinking we should go to the Halloween party on the first night—and look around for evidence while we're there!" she suggested.

"That's a good idea," Sandia replied. "That way, we can make observations without drawing attention."

"I already have my costume picked out," Evelyn said. "I'm going to be a werewolf!"

"I'm going dressed as a mad scientist!" Sandia chimed in, making a crazy face.

The girls all laughed.

"I'm going as a zombie," Treeka announced. She stretched

her arms out in front of herself and dropped her head down.

"I'm going as a skeleton," Mattie grinned.

"And I'll go as a witch," said Ariana, adding an evil cackle for good measure.

They all laughed again.

"This is gonna be a blast!" Sandia beamed.

The crosswalk light turned green, and they crossed the street to finish distributing the flyers. Twenty minutes later, they handed out their last flyer and headed home to start planning their top-secret mission to infiltrate the Sanders Farm, cleverly disguised as trick-or-treaters.

9

HALLOWEEN PARTY

*I*t was the first day of the Sanders Halloween party, and the girls were bursting with excitement.

Sandia the mad scientist, Treeka the zombie, Evelyn the werewolf, Ariana the witch, and Mattie the skeleton were ready for a night of adventure!

They had arrived at the Old Mill before the official start time so they could help hang the banner Ariana had created before people started to arrive.

Mark Sanders retrieved a ladder and set it up on the front patio. He climbed up the ladder and began to nail the banner in place.

"It looks great!" Molly Sanders hollered from across the picnic area, which was strung with tiny orange lights. The girls helped Molly by lighting candles inside two dozen Jack-o'-lanterns that Molly and Mark had carved for this special occasion. Bales of hay surrounded a dance floor and large punch bowls were filled with various flavors of Sanders Cider.

"Everything sure does look wonderful!" Ariana said to Molly.

"And spooky!" Treeka added.

"Why thank you," said Molly. "And thank you all for your help with setting things up. It's been quite a busy week. In addition to getting ready for tonight and tomorrow night's party, we've also been launching our new line of fizzy apple cider beverages. Would you girls like to try some?"

"Oh yes," said the girls, in unison.

They helped themselves to bottled fizzy drinks in large tubs of ice while Molly busied herself applying labels to some glass jars filled with green gooey stuff. One of the labels had the word "Brains" written on it. Treeka reached over and picked up the jar to examine it.

"Brains!" she moaned as she pretended to eat it.

Mark finished hanging the banner and climbed down off the ladder to take a look at it.

"Well done, Ariana! You've outdone yourself," said Mark.

Ariana thanked him. She was very happy to hear that the Sanders liked her work. Getting paid to do what she loved was amazing to her. Having a happy client made it even better.

Mark entered the main building and held the door open for Ariana and her friends.

"Would you like to try some of the other stuff we're serving tonight?" he asked.

"Absolutely!" Treeka answered for them all.

Mark handed out samples of Sanders Farm products, as well as Halloween-themed finger food and treats. It was all delicious.

"Have as much as you'd like," Mark said. "People should start arriving soon. I'm going to go finish up a few last-minute things."

"Mind if I show my friends around?" Ariana asked.

Sandia shot her a look of approval.

"Sure! Have a look around," he replied, as he walked into one of the other buildings.

The girls were suddenly alone in the decorated picnic area.

"Now's our chance to do some detective work," said Sandia. "Ariana, where is the cellar where you saw the ghost?"

"Follow me," said Ariana, as she led them to the cellar door of the old stone mill house.

When they arrived at the door, a newly painted sign above it said, "For those brave enough to enter the Haunted Mill, enjoy Bobbing for Apples."

"Looks like part of the party will be in the cellar," noted Evelyn, as Ariana opened the door and the girls peered down into the entrance.

Once, again, the cellar was pitch black. Evelyn reached into her pocket and pulled out her multitool and turned on its mini LED flashlight.

"I knew you'd be prepared!" laughed Ariana. "Where were you when I needed you, huh?" she teased.

Evelyn smiled and just shrugged. "Maybe we should all start carrying flashlights if we're going to be doing a lot of detec- tivey things from now on," she said, prompting the others to chuckle and nod in agreement.

"Sign me up," said Treeka.

Evelyn led the way and shined her flashlight ahead as they made their way into the cellar entrance.

The others followed her cautiously.

"Here's the light switch," Ariana whispered, as she flipped it on. Like before, the single, dim bulb turned on, barely illuminating only part of the cellar. The girls walked down the stairs and looked around. The cellar had been cleaned up a bit. There were fewer cobwebs, but it still felt damp and had a musty smell to it.

"You weren't kidding about this place being spooky," Mattie commented.

Ariana nodded.

"That's the old apple press," Ariana whispered loudly, as though she didn't want to summon the ghost again.

They slowly approached the old machine. Evelyn shined her flashlight on it.

As they drew closer, Evelyn leaned down and touched the axle on the large cast iron wheel. She rubbed her fingers together and sniffed her fingertips. "Interesting," she said.

Just then, Treeka called out.

"Hey guys, come look over here. Big plastic jars of something."

The others came to look.

"Calcium chloride," Treeka said, reading the labels on the jars to the others.

"Calcium chloride is a food additive," said Sandia. "It's used for flavoring, pickling, and thickening food."

"That makes sense," said Ariana. "The Sanders create lots of food products made from apples."

The door to the cellar flung open abruptly. "Down here!" a man announced, startling the girls.

Two sets of footsteps trampled loudly down the cellar stairs. The girls turned toward the stairs just as two men came into view.

The girls froze in place, afraid they had been caught spying!

But as the men came down the stairs, the girls could see that the men were carrying two large aluminum basins.

"Let's set these up over there!" one of the men said.

Suddenly, he caught a glimpse of the girls huddled around the old apple press.

"Oh, hi!" he said warmly.

"Hi," the girls replied.

"We're here to set up the apple bobbing station!" he said, gesturing to a crate of apples stacked nearby. He and the other man set down the basins on the cellar floor.

"I'll go fetch the hose while you get the towels," said one of the men to the other. They headed back up the stairs and left.

The girls all looked at each other. There was no way they could continue to investigate the ghost incident with an audience.

10

PANDEMONIUM

*T*he girls could hear sounds coming from outside. Guests were starting to arrive for the party. Music began to play. The roar of laughter and excited chatter filled the air.

"Maybe we should head back upstairs," Sandia suggested.

Ariana shrugged. Sandia was right. Now was not the time to collect the data they needed. "Let's go join the party!"

The girls headed up the cellar stairs to participate in the festivities.

From the looks of it, the Halloween party was already a smash hit!

"I'm guessing there are about 200 people here already!" Mattie observed.

Most of the guests were in costume. There were traditional, scary costumes, like vampires and witches, and characters from popular television shows and movies, and some that were impossible to identify or just plain goofy, like a kid dressed as a box of cereal.

"So, what's our plan now?" asked Evelyn.

"I say we just have fun tonight," Ariana suggested. "We can come back tomorrow during the day—when it's light—to search for more clues."

"It's Apple Bobbing time!" someone announced with a loud-speaker, easily heard over the noise of the crowed.

"To the old cellar!" someone else commanded.

"Oooh, that sounds fun!" said Sandia. "Let's go back down and bob for apples!"

"I'm not really sure what bobbing entails," Treeka admitted.

"You know those big basins those guys lugged down into the cellar?" Evelyn asked.

"Yeah," replied Treeka.

"They fill those with water and dump a bunch of apples into it." Evelyn explained.

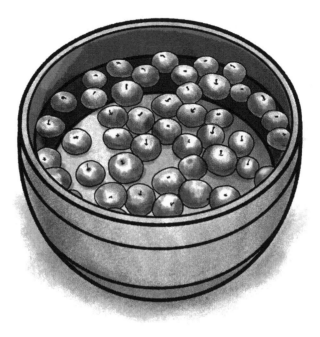

"The apples are less dense than water, so they float on the surface," Sandia added.

"Then you stick your face in the water and try to bite one of the apples without using your hands," Evelyn continued.

"That sounds disgusting," Treeka said.

"The sign says the winner gets a free jar of apple cinnamon dill chutney," said Mattie.

"Okay, I'm in," Treeka said.

"Yay!" Sandia rejoiced, grabbing Treeka by her zombie arm and pulling her toward the cellar door. The others followed close behind as they merged into the crowd of guests heading down into the cellar.

The cellar was crowded with people in costume, all having a great time. Cheers erupted every time someone dunked their head into the basin.

Suddenly, the room turned cold. It felt like the temperature dropped twenty degrees!

Ariana gasped. "That's exactly what I felt right before the ghost appeared!" she whispered to her friends in a raspy tone.

Ariana looked across the room at the apple press just as the pulleys attached to it began to move.

Ka-chung, Ka-chung

"That's the same sound as before!" Ariana remembered.

No one else in the cellar seemed to notice the drop in temperature or the sound of the apple press coming to life.

Ariana motioned to her friends to follow her as she walked toward the press. As they approached it, the room began to fill with an eerie, glowing fog.

And then, just like before, the terrifying, ghostly apparition appeared. All of the guests stopped and looked, as though mesmerized by the phantom, confused by what they were seeing.

"GET OUT! GET OUT!" it shrieked.

Screams filled the cellar. Everyone scrambled to get out as fast as they could! Including STEAMTeam 5!

Well, everyone except for Ariana, that is. She was the last person left standing in the cellar. She stood alone, face-to-face with the ghostly apparition. And it was coming straight for her.

Ariana's trained artist eye had noticed something. Ariana smiled broadly and began to laugh.

11

CALCIUM CHLORIDE

*A*riana stood alone in the cellar, smiling and unafraid, as she closely examined the ghostly vision of Jennylou Livingston's hollow-eyed face and her gracefully billowing white gown.

"Very clever," Ariana said with a smirk.

Ariana jogged up the cellar stairs and went to find her friends in the crowd outside. The music had stopped, and hundreds of people were talking non-stop about having just seen a ghost in the old, haunted cider mill. People were taking selfies with the cellar door in the background, but they kept their distance.

Mark Sanders was trying to calm everybody down. The

guests were too scared to go back inside the cellar, but they were also too excited to leave.

"I saw it with my own eyes!" exclaimed one lady dressed like a pirate.

"I've always known this place was haunted! I knew all along, they weren't just stories," said a teenage boy dressed as a ninja. "Jennylou is back. She's out for revenge!"

"I can assure you, everything is okay," said Mark Sanders, trying to calm the crowd. "Please everybody, please head back down to the apple bobbing station—we've still got lots of jars of chutney to give away. There's nothing to worry about!"

A group of teens laughed at this. "That would be... Nope," one of them said.

"Sorry Mr. Sanders, but I prefer my bones *uncrushed*, thanks," said another.

Mark finally retrieved his loudspeaker and stood on top of one of the picnic tables.

"Attention, everyone!" he said. "Please... everyone!"

The crowd quieted down.

Several people began recording him on their phones and going "live" on social media.

"Please," Mark continued, "stay and enjoy the party.

"But there's a ghost in the cellar!" cried someone in the crowd. "We all saw it!"

Mark paused and looked at Molly. She nodded at him. He lifted his microphone back up to his mouth.

"Perhaps an explanation is in order," he said. An energetic murmur ran through the crowd. They were all focused on what he had to say.

"This mill has a long history, and there have been reports of-- shall we say--'strange happenings' over the years," he began.

"I'm sure many of you have heard rumors," Mark continued. "But tonight, we'd like to set the record straight. Here Molly," he said, gesturing for his wife to take the microphone. "You tell the story better than I do."

Mark handed Molly the microphone and she started to step up onto the picnic table. The crowd murmured and whispered even more at this. What was she going to say?

Ariana had been working her way through the crowd looking for her friends. At last, she found them.

"I think it's a real ghost," Treeka was saying. "I'm certain. I saw it myself. I can't believe I saw an actual ghost! This is awesome!"

"If the universe is a simulation," Mattie said, "the concept of a ghost, in the traditional sense, is meaningless. It would just be a computer program."

"I saw it, too, but I still think it's fake," said Evelyn. "I can't explain it, but I'm sure there's a logical explanation."

"Evelyn is right," Ariana said. The others looked at her in disbelief. "The ghost is fake," Ariana continued. "And I think we can prove it."

Her fellow STEAMTeam members turned to face her, eager for an explanation.

Molly Sanders began to speak over the loudspeaker. "Hello, everybody. Thank you so much for coming out tonight."

"I see some of you have met our, uh, special 'visitor' down in the cellar," Molly continued.

"You mean a GHOST!" yelled someone in the crowd.

"Well, as Mark said," Molly continued, "our Old Cider mill has a very long history. And tonight, I'd like to tell you about something that happened here very long ago. Something terrible."

These words caught Ariana's attention. "I've heard this before," she said, with a skeptical look on her face.

"What about the ghost?" pleaded Sandia. Then she whispered. "How do you know it's fake? How can we prove it?"

The others desperately wanted to know, too, urging Ariana to explain. Ariana looked around. Too many people. "Let's go where we can talk in private. Follow me."

The girls discreetly worked their way out of the crowd as Molly continued her story over the loudspeaker.

"As the legend goes," Molly Sanders began, "this land already had acres and acres of apple trees when Winston Sanders arrived here in the 1850s. He drove his wagon all the way here from Springfield, Ohio. He showed up with his wagon, a set of tools, a brand-new cast iron cider mill, and his new bride. And big dreams!"

When the girls were safely out of earshot of any of the party guests, Ariana stopped and huddled the girls together.

"When I saw the ghost tonight," Ariana began, "I noticed that it was the exact same apparition I saw the other day—not only the same ghost, but literally the exact same vision," Ariana explained.

"The way it moved was identical. The flowing of the gown, everything. It was like I was seeing a video played for a second time," she added.

Treeka raised her eyebrow in Ariana's direction.

"In fact, I'm quite positive that it *is* a video," Ariana clarified.

"What I can't figure out is how the video displays without a screen," she added. She furrowed her brow in frustration.

"Of course!" shouted Sandia, startling them all.

"Calcium chloride!" Sandia exclaimed.

Treeka perked up. She remembered pointing out the large plastic jars of calcium chloride down in the cellar.

"Right O," said Treeka. "Big plastic jars of the stuff, down by the cider press.

"Calcium chloride is used as a food additive," Sandia reminded everyone.

"But it can *also* be mixed with salt to melt ice to produce cooling fog!" Sandia continued.

"That's it!" Ariana exclaimed. "Video can be projected onto fog screens to make really cool effects!"

"Whoa!" said Mattie.

"And when you turn it off," Sandia continued, "the fog dissipates. The screen just... vanishes. Poof!"

"That's a good invention," said Evelyn. "Where would we look for it?"

Sandia thought for a moment. "Well, cold fog is denser than the air around it. So to make a screen out of fog, it must drop down. That means the fog had to have come from somewhere overhead. I'll bet if we look above where the ghost appeared, we'll find a fog machine and a large bin of ice."

Ariana chimed in, "... and a video projector hidden somewhere on the opposite side of the room!"

Ariana paused for a moment and closed her eyes to think.

"But I wonder how the ghost video was activated," she wondered.

"The apple press started up just before the ghost appeared both times," Evelyn noted.

"I pulled a lever just before I saw the ghost the first time," Ariana said. "I thought that maybe the old machine had conjured up the spirit after decades of silence."

"The mill hasn't been silent for decades," Evelyn said. "It's been maintained recently. I found fresh grease on it."

"It seems that Molly Sanders lied to me about the press not working," said Ariana. "But why?"

Ariana looked up from their huddle to see Mark and Molly Sanders beyond the crowd, standing on the picnic table. Molly was still telling the crowd the same ghost story she had told Ariana over cups of cider.

"So, they rigged the apple press to fake a ghost?" Evelyn asked.

"We need to test our hypothesis," Sandia said, "before we draw any conclusions."

"Back to the cellar?" Mattie asked.

"Back to the cellar!" Sandia answered.

With the crowd's attention focused on Molly as she told the story, *the Legend of Jennylou Livingston*, the girls quietly sneaked back down into the cellar. They were on a mission to find the hidden projector!

If anybody could find a false panel or concealed object, it was Treeka. Puzzles and magic tricks were one of her specialties.

After less than a minute of hunting, she found something.

"Ta-da!" Treeka proclaimed, pointing to a wooden cask on a high shelf. The cask had a two-inch wide hole in it and, if you looked closely, you could see a wire running down the wall behind it.

"I'm no barrel expert," Treeka said, "but I'm pretty sure barrels aren't supposed to have holes in them and they're not electric."

"Good eye!" said Mattie. "I never would have noticed that."

"Now where's that fog machine?" Evelyn asked.

The girls looked above where the ghost had appeared, as Sandia had suggested.

"What's that?" Mattie asked, pointing to a long PVC tube poking out of the ceiling above them, concealed by one of the beams.

Without answering, Evelyn raced up the cellar stairs. The others all looked at each other, and suddenly started running upstairs after her.

Evelyn led them into the store, which was located directly above the cellar in the old stone building. They all began searching feverishly for the other end of the PVC tube.

"I found it!" cried Sandia from behind the counter.

The others scurried around the counter to get a look for themselves. And there it was.

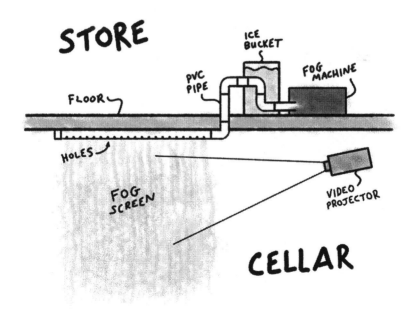

"A fog machine," Sandia said.

Next to the fog machine, there was a large bin of ice, a bag of salt, and a large, plastic jar of calcium chloride.

Running out of the fog machine was a wide PVC tube used to direct the fog down through the floor and into the cellar below. The fog exited the tube through a series of small holes, creating a "screen" of fog.

Treeka's zombie makeup face smiled as she put her hand on Ariana's shoulder. "Congratulations, Ariana. There's your ghost."

12

MEDIA FRENZY

*M*attie turned to Ariana. "So, are you going to ask the Sanders why they pretended the cellar is haunted?"

Ariana hesitated. "I'm not really sure how to ask."

"Maybe something like, 'What's up with the fake ghost?'" Evelyn proposed.

"Let's go see what's happening outside," said Ariana. "I can hear Molly. It sounds like she's getting close to the end of her story."

The girls emerged from the building. The crowd was still paying rapt attention to Molly. But now, there were bright lights shining on Mark and Molly. The local news station's camera crew had arrived!

"Wow, this is really blowing up," Evelyn noted.

Molly was still speaking over the loudspeaker.

"Some folks say Becky had a particularly lovely garden the following spring," she said.

The crowd gasped at this.

"I know how this story ends, said Ariana. "Let's go talk to Mr. and Mrs. Sanders."

STEAMTeam 5 walked through the crowd, making their way to the front where Molly was speaking, with Mark standing next to her.

"Now, I'm sure you all have lots of questions about our 'ghost,'" Molly said with a big smile.

The crowd erupted with a flurry of questions. The news reporter and her camera crew seized the moment and moved in to interview the Sanders.

"What can you tell us about the ghost that people reported seeing here tonight?" asked the aggressive reporter, thrusting a microphone into Molly's face.

Molly was about to answer, when a voice nearby called out, "It's not a ghost. It's fake."

The news reporter stopped and turned toward the voice. It was Ariana, standing there in her witch costume, suddenly frozen as the lights and news video camera focused on her.

"And who's this?" asked the reporter, turning her microphone to Ariana. "A young lady in a witch costume. Did you see the ghost tonight?"

Ariana just stared into the camera, frozen like a deer in headlights. She felt her face growing hot, like the whole world was watching her. She swallowed hard and finally managed to squeak out, "Um... the ghost. It's... it's...."

Treeka jumped in to rescue her friend, sticking her zombie-makeup face right between Ariana and the news cameras and microphone.

"It's fake! The ghost is fake!" said Treeka, confidently. "An elaborate hoax by greedy real estate developers to scare away customers and force the Sanders to sell their land so they can build luxury condominiums!"

Both the Sanders and news crew looked very confused. Evelyn covered her mouth with one of her hairy werewolf paws to keep herself from laughing.

"Luxury... what?" asked Mark.

"I don't know about any of that real estate stuff," said Molly, "but our new Jennylou Livingston Ghost Attraction looks like it's going to be a real crowd-pleaser!"

"Attraction?" Ariana asked.

"Hi, Ariana!" said Molly. "Yes! Like they have at amusement parks. We created it as the centerpiece of our annual Halloween party," Molly said, beaming with pride.

"Huh..." was all Ariana could muster.

"What do you think? Pretty scary, huh?" Molly continued, still smiling ear-to-ear.

"I built the fog screen, and Mark did a great job with the video. That's me in a white wig, you know... *GET OUT!*" she said, mimicking the Jennylou ghost, but with a laugh.

"Scary indeed, from the looks of this crowd," said the news reporter with an overly big smile.

The reporter turned and looked directly into the camera. "There you have it, lots of fun for the whole family and a super scary ghost attraction. The party's going until midnight tonight and tomorrow night, 6:00pm to midnight. But come early! If tonight's any indication, tomorrow night might draw ten times as many people! Reporting live from Sanders Farms Old Cider Mill, this is Sarah Broche. Back to you, Ron."

The reporter maintained her perfect smile until the camera operator gave a signal and the bright lights turned off.

Her smile vanished, and she nodded at the Sanders. "Good

luck." She then turned to her camera crew. "That's a wrap. Let's roll." And they were off.

"Can you believe it? The news!" said Molly, to no one in particular, slightly stunned by the success of the night.

Molly turned to Ariana. "Did you like the ghost? We worked so hard on it."

"I... I don't understand," said Ariana. "Why did you tell me the apple press hadn't worked in years? Why didn't you tell me you made a ghost?"

"Oh, that's part of the act," said Molly. "I've been practicing my lines for weeks!

"In fact, when you dropped by last week, you were my very first live audience! Did you like the story? Most of it's true, you know," Molly continued, speaking so fast that she could barely catch her breath.

"Oh, by the way, I'm so sorry I didn't get a chance to show you Jennylou before I got called away! You had left by the time I returned, so I never got to show you."

"Oh..." said Ariana. "I actually, um, found it. The lever said, 'pull me.'"

"Oh, good heavens!" said Molly. "That must've been a fright. I hope it didn't startle you."

"Who me?" said Ariana. "Nah, of course n... well, okay, it

scared the living daylights out of me, to be honest. I thought it... was..." Ariana paused, embarrassed to admit that she had been fooled.

Molly's eyes opened wide. "Oh my, did you think it was... real?" She hugged Ariana, who managed a slightly embarrassed nod.

"That's wonderful!" cried Molly. This confused Ariana.

"You have no idea how happy that makes me, Ariana. You know, I wanted to get your professional opinion on the attraction before showing it to the public. We've never created anything 'theatrical' before. You being scared is the biggest compliment we could ever receive! I mean, you're a pro!"

Molly hugged Ariana again and then turned away to talk to other people who had been waiting patiently. Mark had already been speaking to others.

By this time, the whole crowd knew that "Jenny"—as people had started calling the ghost—was to become a regular attraction at Sanders Farm, during tours they would be giving year-round.

THE GIRLS SAT IN SILENCE ON THE PATIO AT THE SANDERS Cider mill, sipping on fizzy cider. A large fire blazed in a nearby fire pit. Evelyn and Mattie were warming their hands near it.

Ariana was spinning her witch hat with her finger.

About every fifteen minutes, a new partygoer in the cellar pulled the lever, activating "Jenny," and sending new crowds of delighted party-goers into thrills as they ran out of the cellar screaming.

"Get 'em, Jennylou," said Treeka.

Evelyn pointed at Mattie's skeleton costume—it was all black with glow-in-the-dark bones. "You need to eat more."

"You need to shave," said Mattie, looking at Evelyn's werewolf cheek fur.

The girls all laughed.

They felt weird about their whole ghost hunt.

"I guess sometimes a mystery isn't a mystery," said Ariana.

"It's a mystery until you figure out it's not one," Sandia said.

The girls nodded in silent agreement.

"We might sometimes get a little ahead of ourselves, I guess, but you know what?" Sandia said. "We're pretty good detectives, if I do say so myself."

The girls nodded again, with more enthusiasm this time.

"We should solve more of them," Sandia concluded.

"Anybody got any mysteries?" asked Evelyn.

Everybody tried to think of something. After a while, Mattie spoke up.

"Well, now that you mention it," she said. "There's this weird, sweet smell in my backyard sometimes. You can smell it when it rains, or sometimes when the wind blows. I have no idea what's causing it."

The others all leaned in a bit.

Sandia pulled her notepad out of her lab coat pocket and clicked the top of her ballpoint pen, then looked up to Mattie with a grin.

"Tell us more."

THE END

FREE ACTIVITY GUIDE

To receive a free .PDF ebook copy of our STEAMTeam 5 Activity book, please send an email to info@steamteam5.com and mention the title of this book.

Made in the USA
Middletown, DE
11 May 2020